To make your dolls, you will need:

crayons

hole puncher

scissors

16 ½" brass fasteners

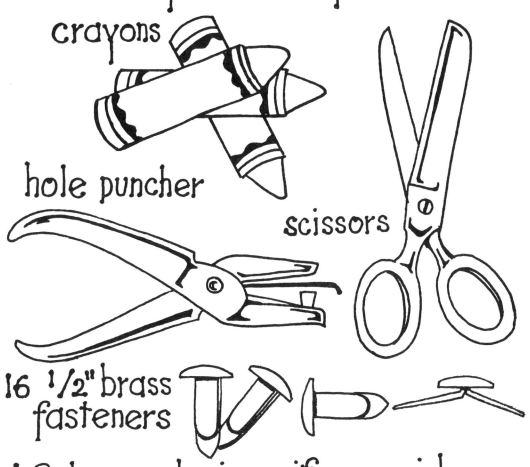

1. Color each piece if you wish.
2. Cut each body piece carefully.
3. Punch out holes at circles.
4. Match up holes by letters.
5. Attatch by putting brass fasteners through matched holes and spreading posts until flat.

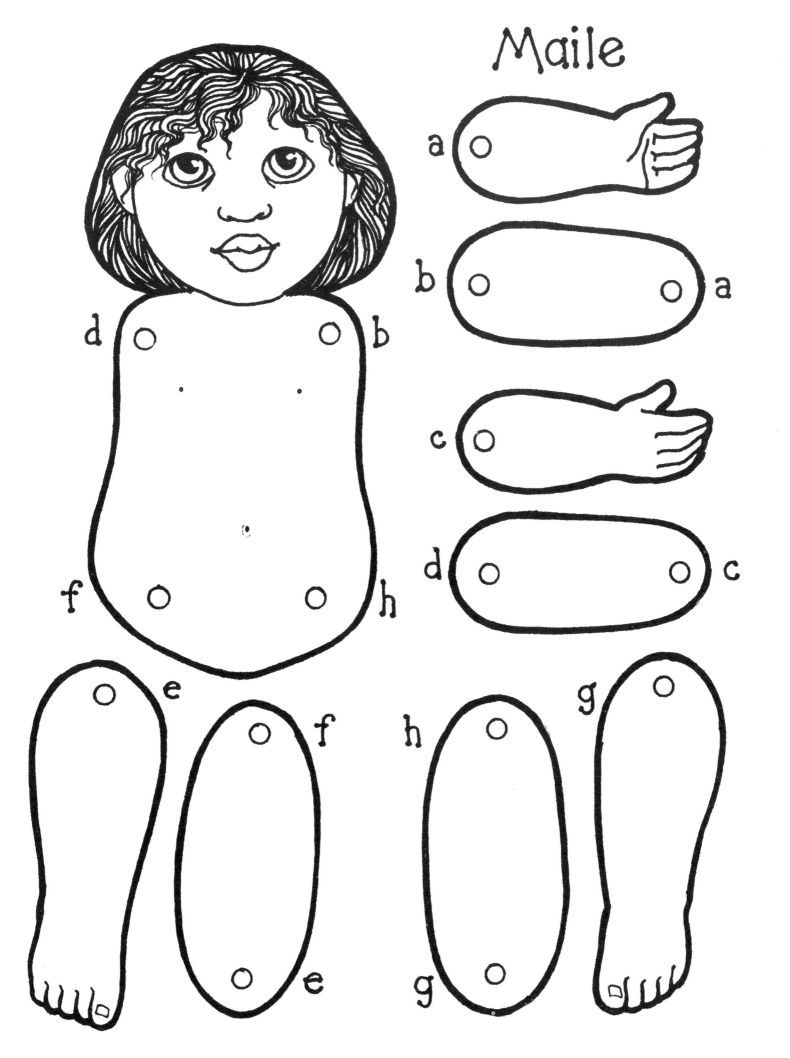

Maile

aloha wear

hula kahiko

CUT HERE TO HERE

at the beach

play time

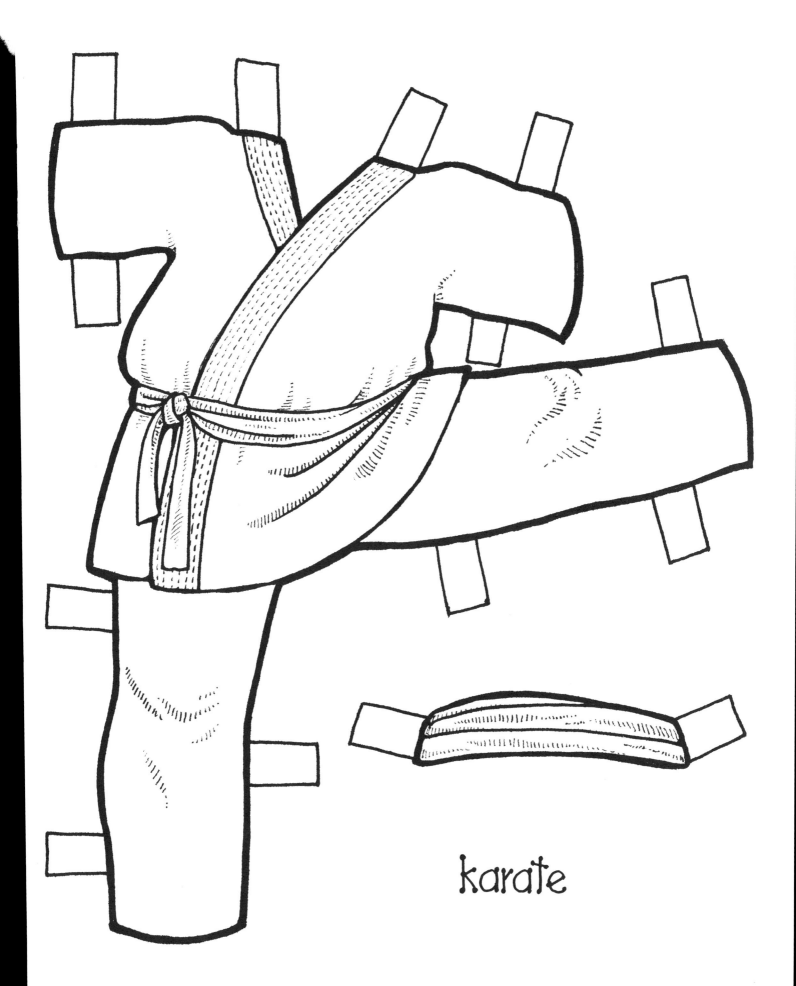

karate

karate

play time

at the beach

hula kahiko

CUT FROM HERE TO HERE

aloha wear

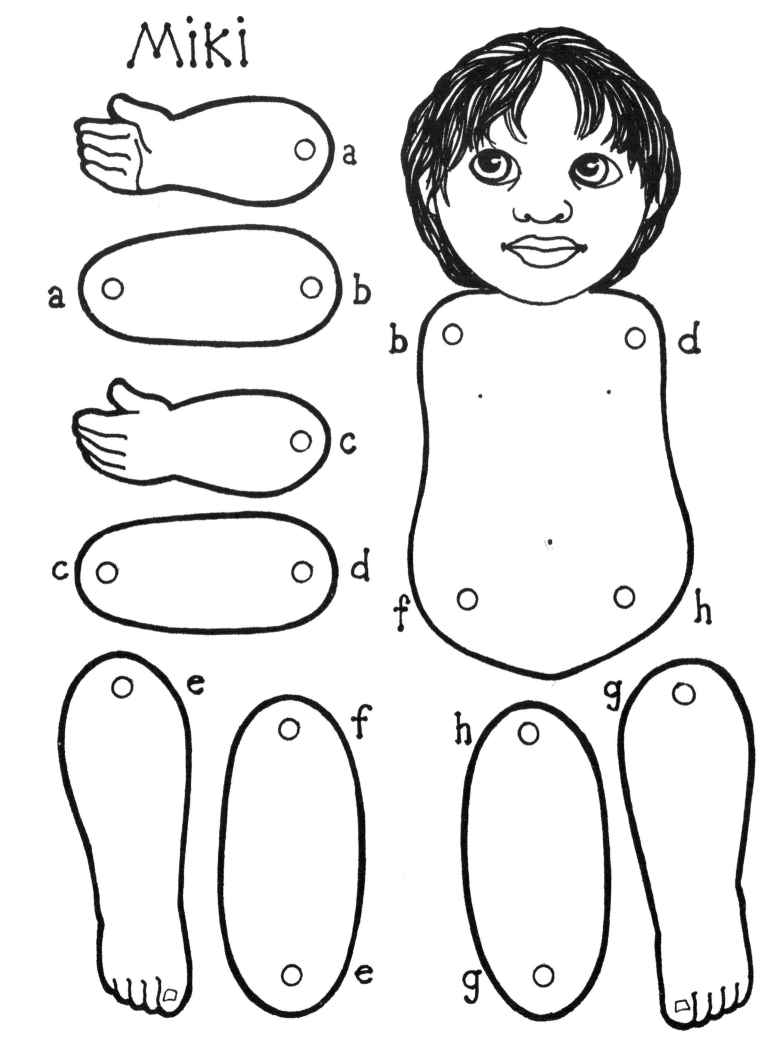

To make your doll clothes:

1. Color each piece.
2. Cut each piece carefully along the thick black line, being carefully not to cut off tabs.
3. Put outfit on doll. Bend tabs back to hold in place.
   If you are very active, you may want to hold your doll's clothes in place with paper clips.
4. Have fun!

Try to make your own paper doll clothes. Use your imagination. These dolls can dance, sit, party, play, and ...